WINTER FOX

by JENNIFER BRUTSCHY

illustrated by ALLEN GARNS

ALFRED A. KNOPF New York

THIS IS A BORZOI BOOK PUBLISHED BY ALFRED A. KNOPF, INC.

Published in the United States of America by Alfred A. Knopf, Inc., New York, and
simultaneously in Canada by Random House of Canada Limited, Toronto. Distributed by
Random House, Inc., New York.

Book design by Mina Greenstein
Manufactured in the United States of America   1 2 3 4 5 6 7 8 9 10

Library of Congress Cataloging-in-Publication Data
Brutschy, Jennifer
Winter Fox / by Jennifer Brutschy ; illustrations by Allen Garns.
p.   cm.   Summary: During a very cold winter, Rosemary tries to protect her pet rabbit
from a hungry fox.
ISBN 0-679-81524-4 (trade)   ISBN 0-679-91524-9 (lib. bdg.)
[1. Rabbits—Fiction. 2. Foxes—Fiction. 3. Winter—Fiction.]   I. Garns, Allen, ill.   II. Title
PZ7.B8288Wi   1993   [E]—dc20   92-33467

To Marc
        who listens
and the fox
        who inspires
                —J. B.

To Diane
                —A. G.

Deep into winter, when the air was sharp and biting, Papa brought me a soft white rabbit. I named her Annabelle, which was the most beautiful name I had ever heard.

Papa built her a wooden hutch, which he said would keep her warm and dry.

I helped pound in the nails and carry the hutch to a sun-warmed spot near the barn.

Every morning and every evening I checked on Annabelle. I gave her clean straw for her bedding and fresh water to drink.

She and I shared the carrot sticks from my lunch. Mama saw me once, but she didn't say a word.

"Remember to close Annabelle's hutch when you leave her," Papa reminded me. I knew he'd seen a fox the night before. I had heard him telling Mama about it when they thought I was sound asleep.

I latched Annabelle's hutch that evening and watched
carefully for the fox as I crossed the snowy field.
I was sure the fox was as big as a tiger and as strong as a

bear. When I thought about it, I got so scared that I ran like
a deer across the field.

The snow made crunching sounds wherever my boots
landed, and the tree branches looked like claws in the deep
winter dusk.

Back in the warm, cozy kitchen I just laughed when Mama asked what had scared me so. Nothing seemed spooky anymore.

During the next week the weather turned mean. Threads of ice hung from the roof of the barn, and Papa worried about our chickens.

When the weather is cold, he said, a fox will grow daring. It will enter the yard in search of food. And a crafty fox has no trouble carrying off a chicken or two.

Chickens were okay, but Annabelle was special, and I worried about her alone in her hutch.

One bitterly cold afternoon I came home from school to discover Annabelle was missing. "Drink some hot cocoa before you go out looking," Mama said. But I wasn't cold or thirsty. I just wanted to find Annabelle.

I searched until dark, calling her name, peering under thick white clumps of snowy bushes.

I didn't notice how cold I was until the sun began to set and the wind began to howl. It sounded like the cry of a hungry animal searching for my gentle Annabelle in the winter dusk.

After dinner Papa took his rifle from the rack in the shed. It scared me a little. "What are you doing, Papa?"

"Just finish your dinner, Rosemary," he said.

I felt a shivery thrill go through me because I knew exactly what he was doing. He was going out to hunt the fox.

"Can I come with you, Papa? Please?"

He looked at Mama, then nodded. "Bundle up tight. It's a frosty moon, my girl." That meant the moon was full and we would be able to see forever across the deep, polished snow.

Outside, everything shone white. Our wheat fields were
hidden under the snow's crust, and the stars hung clear and
close.
In the cold my teeth chattered.

Papa didn't look cold. He stood so still I could hardly see him breathing.

Suddenly, I felt Papa move beside me. I looked where he was looking. Something was prowling across the snow.

As it came closer, I could see it was the fox. In the moonlight it looked winter-thin, butterscotch-pale. Its coat was ragged, its body lean and hungry.

My stomach felt hollow as I watched the fox sniff the barren snow. It needed food. Papa raised his gun.

"No!" I shouted.

My voice frightened the fox, and we watched it run swiftly toward the row of trees in the distance.

Papa lowered his gun and turned to face me. "You know he took Annabelle?" The stubble on his chin looked rough, like stalks of wheat we would harvest later in the year. But his eyes were gentle and questioning.

"I know, Papa."

I didn't say anything else and neither did Papa. But I thought about how thin and alone that fox had looked. How hungry it must have been on such a cold winter night.

I cried onto Papa's shoulder, not sure if I was crying for Annabelle or for the fox.

Papa put his big mittened paw on my arm. "Let's go warm up, Rosie," he said, and we stomped quietly back to the house through a silent field of snow.